There Is a
DRAGON
Under MY Door

Darren Sylte

There Is a Dragon Under My Door

Copyright © 2018 Darren Sylte.

iUniverse books may be ordered through booksellers or by contacting:

iUniverse
1663 Liberty Drive
Bloomington, IN 47403
www.iuniverse.com
1-800-Authors (1-800-288-4677)

ISBN: 978-1-5320-4799-2 (sc)
ISBN: 978-1-5320-4800-5 (e)

Library of Congress Control Number: 2018904852

Print information available on the last page.

iUniverse rev. date: 05/02/2018

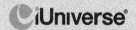

To Zoey
I'm Fred
your Grandson
good
friend
Hope
enjoys this

There Is a
DRAGON
under MY Door

There is a Dragon under my door.
And I know it.

My mom says that I am being silly, but I know he is there.

Every night when I go to bed
I can hear him breathing...
there, under my door.

Mom tucks me into bed every night and closes my bedroom door. At first it is quiet, but soon I can hear him... there, under my door.

Every night he comes back and sits outside of my bedroom door, just waiting.

I try to ignore that dragon under my door, but he just won't go away.

I pull the blankets up over my head.
But still, he is there.

I bury my head under my pillow, hoping that he will be gone when I peek out.

But still, he is there.

I have even tried to hum a song
to myself, any song... just to make
some noise and drown out that
dragon sound under my door.

Finally, I doze off to sleep; I just can't fight it anymore.

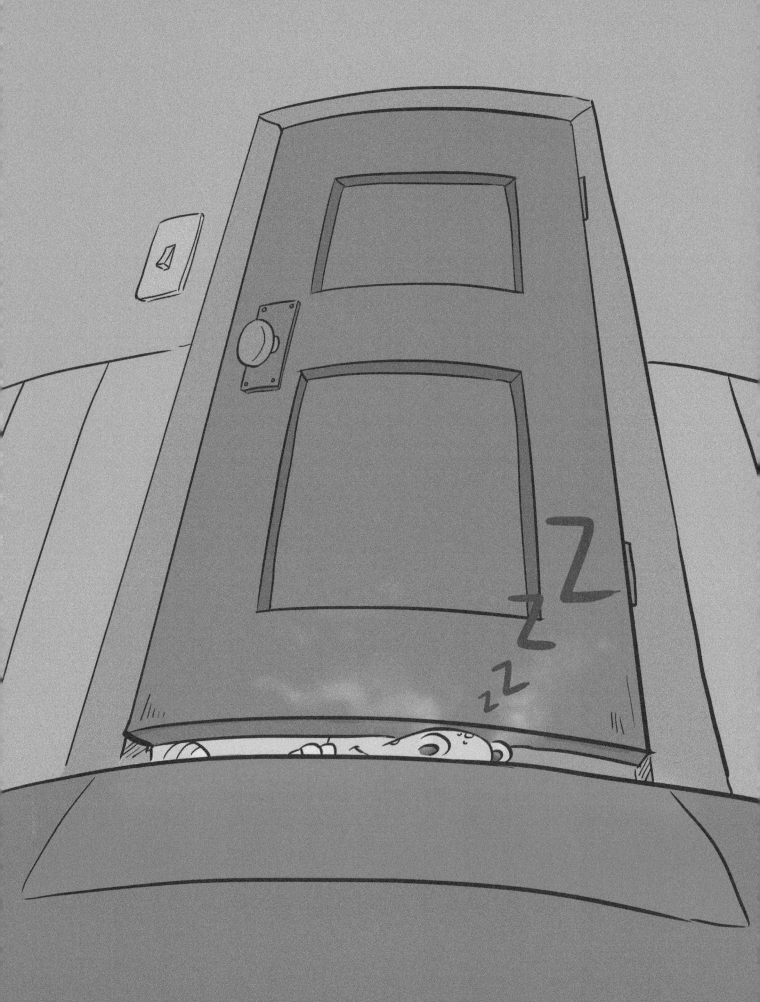

That dragon under my door.

When I wake, I quietly walk toward my door... wondering if that dragon is still there, under the door.

Slowly, I open the door and there on the floor is my old dog, in a deep sleep, with a great snore.

My brave old dog had chased that dragon away from under my door.

What a wonderful chore.

CPSIA information can be obtained
at www.ICGtesting.com
Printed in the USA
LVHW07s0125010618
579191LV00010B/19/P

9 781532 047992